WHEN THE MOON IS NEW

A SEMINOLE INDIAN STORY

Laura Bannon
Author-illustrator

ALBERT WHITMAN & COMPANY   CHICAGO, ILLINOIS

In Florida, great lakes of shallow water are covered with saw grass. Small islands crowded with palm trees dot the grassy waters. And sometimes, under the trees, the brown roofs of a Seminole Indian camp may be seen.

This is the story of a Seminole girl who lives in one of these camps. Her house is called a 'chickee'....

Standard Book Number 8075-8896-2
Library of Congress Card 53-7925
© 1953 by Laura Bannon
Published simultaneously in Canada by George J. McLeod, Ltd., Toronto
Lithographed in the United States
Fourth Printing 1969

WHEN THE MOON IS NEW

The air was full of mystery. Little Rainbow Jumper could feel it all around her. No one talked about it out loud. But the grown-ups smiled and whispered to each other.

Rainbow watched Mother Jumper. She was combing her long black hair over a cardboard shaped like the brim of a hat.

Mother was seeing something not before her eyes. She was smiling a secret thought.

"What are you smiling about?" Rainbow asked. "I can tell there is a mystery in our camp."

Only Rainbow didn't really say *mystery*. She said *we-kiva* which means mystery in the Seminole language. Rainbow said everything in Seminole. Why not? She was a little Seminole Indian.

Mother Jumper put a net over her hair, then tilted the brim, hair and all, to one side. She straightened the fifty strings of beads she wore around her neck. How pretty Mother looked when she smiled like that!

"Please tell me about the mystery," Rainbow coaxed.

Mother picked up the basket she was weaving. "Be patient, little one," she said. "When the moon is new you will know about the mystery."

Rainbow sat swinging her legs from the platform of the *chickee*. Last night the moon was as round as a melon, she remembered. Many nights would pass before it shrank to nothing, then climbed the sky again, a bright thin bow.

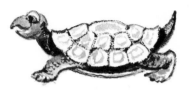

"But Mother, that is a long time to wait," Rainbow said. "How can I wait so long to find out about the mystery?"

"Time moves like the slow turtle because your hands are idle," said Mother. "You will forget time if you keep your hands busy. Go help Grandmother make the *sofkee*. Father will come home from the big hunt any day now. He will be very hungry. He must find *sofkee* in the kettle."

Rainbow walked slowly to the cookhouse that stood in the middle of the quiet camp ground. If only she lived in a camp full of noise, like the camp of Aunt Liddy Gopher! Cousins of every size lived at the Gopher camp. They were always screaming and laughing while they played at their games.

Best of all a darling baby cousin lived there, Little Willie Gopher.

Grandmother Jumper came carrying a big kettle of water to the cookhouse. Her long skirts swept the ground like a gentle wind. Grandmother wore one hundred strings of beads around her neck. They were piled from her shoulders to her chin.

Like a big bumblebee she hummed a song as she walked. Was she thinking about the mystery too?

On the ground of the cookhouse, heavy logs lay with their ends together like the spokes of a wheel. Grandmother pushed them in closer to feed the fire at the center. When it flamed up she stood the black kettle in the fire.

Rainbow walked with Grandmother to the plat-

form where food was made ready for the *sofkee*. "Why are you so happy?" she asked.

Grandmother just kept on cutting deer meat into small chunks.

Rainbow peeled yellow skins off the yams. "I can tell we have a big mystery in our camp," she said. "Mother says I'll know about it when the moon is new. How can I wait so long?"

"It is worth waiting for," said Grandmother Jumper. "And when it comes it will keep your hands busy."

"The wait would be easy if I could visit the Gopher camp," Rainbow said.

"Yes," said Grandmother. "There time races like the rabbit before the panther. There is much to do at the Gopher Camp. You could help Aunt Liddy Gopher care for Little Willie."

Excitement showed in Rainbow's black eyes. "I could swing  him in his hammock. And now I'm big enough to carry him." Rainbow put the knife down. "I'll finish sewing my new skirt so I can wear it if I go visiting," she said.

"First we finish making the *sofkee*," said Grandmother.

Rainbow shelled lima beans while Grandmother pounded corn. Then with a big wooden spoon she stirred corn, meat and vegetables into the kettle.

At last Rainbow could work on the skirt. She ran to the *chickee* of Big Grandmother Jumper. Big Grandmother was very old. She was Grandmother's mother. The new skirt was being made on her sewing machine.

Oh, dear! Big Grandmother was using the machine herself. She spun the wheel with one wrinkled brown hand and guided a long strip of cloth with the other.

Rainbow climbed onto the platform of the *chickee*. She stooped over and spoke clearly into the old one's ear.

"Mother says I'll know about the mystery when the moon is new. That is a long time to wait. Grandmother says time will race like the fast rabbit if I visit the Gopher camp. If my new skirt were finished I could wear it."

The sewing machine slowed down.

Big Grandmother patted Rainbow's cheek and

thought about this. The old one was very wise. She decided almost everything that had to be decided in the Jumper camp.

At last Big Grandmother spoke: "Your Father has been gone on the big hunt many days. He will return soon and your Uncle Whirlwind Gopher will be with him. You could ride to the Gopher camp with Uncle Whirlwind. Yes, you could help Aunt Liddy and learn to be a good visitor."

"I'll take care of Little Willie," said Rainbow.

Big Grandmother nodded her head. "After your father stretches the skins from the hunt he will take them, along with the baskets and skirts we make, to the white man's store. On the way home he could stop at the Gopher camp for you.

"Then I can go?" asked Rainbow.

"Yes, you will make the visit. It is best so. But our hearts will be empty without you," the old one added.

Rainbow spun on one heel until her cape and skirt ballooned out like a striped top. "I'll rock Little Willie to sleep," she sang. "I'll carry him with me while I play."

"Your new skirt must be finished by sunset," said Big Grandmother. "You will be ready to go whenever the men get back."

Rainbow stood on a crate to reach her bundle of sewing. It was tucked high on a rafter under the roof. In it were rolls of cloth, long bands made from tiny pieces of bright cotton all sewn together in pretty designs.

"It will be beautiful, won't it, Big Grandmother?" Rainbow bragged. "It won't be made with thousands of pieces like the skirts you make. But it will have many hundreds of pieces."

"We shall see," Big Grandmother answered. "You have yet to finish it." She rummaged through a pile of cotton cloth. "You will need strips of plain cloth to put between the bands of designs," she said.

They laid the bands Rainbow had sewn beside the strips they tore from solid colors. Would they place pink beside the green and yellow design? Would the white rick-rack braid look best over the dark red cloth?

These things decided, Rainbow began to sew the bands together. Now it was beginning to look like a real skirt. By the time the evening sun blazed behind the palm trees the skirt was finished.

Mother and Grandmother and Big Grandmother

held it between them. They turned it inside out to look at the seams. Rainbow heard something not intended for her ears.

Big Grandmother whispered it so loud you could hear it anywhere in camp. "The little one sews as well as many grown women," she said.

Mother and Rainbow ate supper with the Grandmothers at the eating house. They all sat on the floor around the kettle of *sofkee*. Each in turn ate the good food from the large wooden spoon.

Rainbow said, "At the Gopher camp I'll be as busy as the humming bird. But sometimes I'll think about the mystery. Mother says I'll know about it when the moon is new. Grandmother says it will keep my hands busy. Maybe Big Grandmother, too, will give me a hint to carry in my thoughts."

The grown-ups all smiled into each other's eyes.

"I'll give you this hint," said Big Grandmother. "The mystery is about something new, something you will treasure."

Suddenly Rainbow knew the answer to the mystery. They were going to give her a sewing ma-chine for her very own.

The thought itself was enough to make the heart dance. A girl of only seven summers to own a sewing machine! But had not Big Grandmother said, "The little one sews as well as a grown woman"? And all Seminole women owned and treasured sewing machines.

After supper the sky grew dark. Mother hung a canvas across one side of the *chickee* to shut out the sharp wind that blew across the grassy waters. Then she and Rainbow each wrapped themselves in a warm blanket and lay down on the floor to sleep.

Through the open sides of the *chickee* Rainbow watched the Everglade Kite. What a nimble bird! He tumbled down the velvet sky, catching insects.

Barred owls hooted from the old tree down by the cookhouse.

In the marshes big and little frogs came out of their secret hiding places. They had been quiet all day. Now they filled the air with their throbbing.

Rainbow was used to all these noises of the night.

The moon sent its glow of light before it, then peeped over the miles of saw grass. Why! Tonight it had lost some of its roundness. Rainbow was a little closer to owning the new sewing machine.

"I know just how it will be," she thought. "Father will sell all the things in the big city. With the money he will buy a canoe full of fine things. When he gets home he will unload boxes of food and beads and braid and thread and cloth. Last of all, for the big surprise, he will unload the shining new machine.

"I'll seem very surprised," Rainbow decided. "That will make Mother and the Grandmothers happy too."

Rainbow fell asleep and dreamed and smiled. Was she dreaming about the new sewing machine? No. She dreamed she was playing with Little Willie.

Suddenly she woke. A sharp bird call pierced her ear. It whistled again and again through the moonlit night, "Twa-er-ee, twa-er-ee."

Mother was sitting up, listening too. She rose,

took the kerosene lantern down from its hook under the roof and lighted it.

"What is it, Mother?" Rainbow asked.

"The men are coming home from the big hunt," said Mother.

She hurried with the lantern to the cookhouse. Rainbow followed, blinking at the swaying light.

Mother shoved the smoldering ends of the logs closer together so the coals glowed and sent up tongues of fire. She put the kettle of *sofkee* over the blaze. "They'll be as hungry as the alligator," she said.

The sharp bird call was close now. Rainbow and Mother, Grandmother and even Big Grandmother hurried down to the landing of their tiny island. They peered across the water. Out there in the moonlight

they saw two canoes snaking their way through the tall grass.

The women called softly, *"Ha-tee-e-tew-chee hick-chay-hit-es-chay."*

All those sounds together meant, "Glad to see."

Father stood in the back of the first canoe. He pushed with a long pole sending the canoe silently through the shallow water. With a last powerful

push he ran forward, jumped to dry land and pulled the canoe up after him.

"Luck was with you," said Mother. "You bring much game from the hunt."

"Yes," said Father. "But it is good to be home where the smell of *sofkee* fills the air."

Uncle Whirlwind Gopher pulled his canoe up beside Father's. In it, along with the piles of furs, was

a huge alligator he had killed. It sprawled there with eyes staring, claws curled.

Rainbow was glad to leave the bumpy creature behind when she went with the grown-ups to the eating house.

Mother made fry bread and coffee.

Father passed the big wooden spoon filled with *sofkee* to Uncle Whirlwind. "Eat plenty," he said.

The lighted lantern, hanging from a rafter, swayed gently. And with it the black shadow of each person swayed back and forth across the bare wood floor. Rainbow leaned against Father and watched the shadows until her eyes closed and she slept soundly.

When she woke she was alone in her family *chickee*. The morning sun burned a hole in the sky with its brightness.

Had Uncle Whirlwind gone home without her? No. She could hear his booming voice.

Then Mother called, "Wake up, Rainbow. If you are to visit the cousins you must hurry."

Rainbow washed her face, combed her hair, and changed to her pretty new skirt. She ate fish Mother had fried, then stood at the landing saying good-by to her family.

Uncle Whirlwind pushed his canoe into the water. "Hop in, Rainbow," he said.

Rainbow held tight to the bundle of clothing Mother handed her. She stood still as a stone.

"It is time to go," Mother said. "Remember to

hold only respectful words on your tongue. Learn to be a good visitor."

Rainbow just stood and stared at the canoe so filled with the big bull alligator.

Uncle Whirlwind laughed. "Would you rather sit with me or the 'gator?" he asked. Then he picked up Rainbow and carried her past all the scratchy claws to the back end of the canoe.

Rainbow watched her home as the canoe slid away from it. "*Ay-lip-ka-shaw,* good-by," she called.

Soon the Jumper camp ground looked like the hundreds of other tiny islands of palm trees that sat in the great lake of grass.

Uncle Whirlwind guided his canoe through the narrow water paths.

They passed cypress trees that played dead,

standing with their feet in the water. Their chalk white branches made lace against the sky. Air plants, clinging to the branches, drank from the damp air and blossomed in red splashes.

The canoe slid along so silently that long-legged birds, standing up to their feathers in the water, kept on fishing. A great blue heron with his yard-long neck and black bead eyes watched for frogs in the water.

The sun was high now and Rainbow was hungry. "How much further is it to camp?" she asked.

"We'll soon be there," Uncle Whirlwind told her.

The canoe darted through patches of water lilies and giant ferns that stood as tall as Uncle's head.

Small wet mounds covered with violets peeped above the surface of the water. The mounds became islands where enormous morning glories crowded over the pines and palms. Spider lilies fringed the water's edge.

"I would like to pick some flowers for Aunt Liddy," said Rainbow.

Uncle Whirlwind stopped the canoe. While Rainbow picked flowers he whistled, "Twa-er-ee, twa-er-ee."

From an island ahead Rainbow heard the shrill shouts of many children. Dogs barked and a rooster crowed. Aunt Liddy's deep voice shouted, "Glad to see."

Uncle Whirlwind sent the canoe shooting toward

the island. The landing swarmed with children and chickens and dogs and ducks. Aunt Liddy Gopher stood in the middle like a mother hen.

Uncle Whirlwind lifted Rainbow past the big bull 'gator and stood her in the crowd of chattering cousins. There were so many of them. It was hard to tell which were Aunt Liddy's children and which were visitors from other camps.

Rainbow felt shy at first. But then she held the flowers out to Aunt Liddy and said, "For you."

After Aunt Liddy took the flowers she lifted a string of beads from her neck and slipped them over Rainbow's head. "For you," she said.

All the boy cousins crowded around the big 'gator. But the girl cousins crowded around Rainbow and admired her new skirt. She was the oldest girl, she

noticed. That was good. She would be the one to take care of Little Willie.

Where was Little Willie? The small hammock that hung in Aunt Liddy's *chickee* sagged in the middle. Rainbow and the other girls climbed onto the platform and gathered around the plump baby.

He stared at Rainbow with surprised eyes. She dangled her beads in front of him until he laughed.

Before the day was over he was riding happily, like a little brother, on Rainbow's hip. Rainbow was happy too. Now she was part of a big noisy family.

Grandmother Jumper was right. At the Gopher camp time raced like the fast rabbit. There were so many things to do and plenty of noise to hear.

There was the THUMP, THUMP, THUMP of someone pounding corn. SMACK went the arrows against the target when the oldest boys practiced shooting. The roosters CROWED. The hens CACKLED. The pigs GRUNTED. The ducks QUACKED. The dogs BARKED. And the cousins SCREAMED at their games.

Even Little Willie added his voice to all the noise. For he was a part of the games, too, because he rode on Rainbow's hip. And she was always in the middle of everything.

But Rainbow didn't play all the time. After Aunt Liddy scrubbed clothes over a log and rinsed them, Rainbow helped pull the shirts and skirts over bushes so they dried without wrinkles.

The most fun was on the day Aunt Liddy showed the girls how to make dolls to sell at the white man's store.

While Little Willie played in his hammock beside her, Rainbow sewed small Seminole doll dresses on Aunt Liddy's sewing machine. She made dresses for a whole row of dolls.

All this time Uncle Whirlwind was busy caring for the skins and furs from the big hunt. Now the skin of the big 'gator was stretched flat on a board that stood against a tree.

Then one morning Uncle Whirlwind piled the skins and furs in his canoe along with all the dolls. Off he went through the water paths in the saw grass to the white men's city beside the ocean.

He was gone all that night and all the next day.

When the sun set again the noise of the Gopher camp died down. The dogs came back from hunting rabbits in the marshes and lay dozing under

 the *chickees*. Chickens crowded together along the low tree branches.

Rainbow wrapped herself up to her chin in a blanket and lay down on the floor of the visitor's *chickee* with the other girls. For the first time since she came to the Gopher camp she didn't fall asleep at once.

She listened to the sing-song of the insects that make music for each other after sundown. The sky was alight with stars. Why! There was the moon as slim as a reed.

"Are you the old moon, nearly gone?" Rainbow whispered. "Or are you the new moon?"

She had been sleeping too soundly at night to keep track of the moon.

"Soon I'll go home where time moves like the slow turtle," thought Rainbow, "Big Grandmother and Grandmother and Mother and I will all sew on our machines. There will be nothing to listen to but a soft whirr.

"I'll be glad to see Father and Mother and the Grandmothers. But, oh, how can I leave Little Willie? He needs me. Who will carry him through the games? Who will have time to dry his tears when he cries?"

Out across the marsh a red winged blackbird sang out after his bed time, "Twaa-er-ee, twaa-er-ee?" But was that really a blackbird singing?

The quiet of the Gopher camp didn't last long. The dogs began to bark. All the cousins rolled out of their blankets and chattered like the sparrow. They ran to the landing, a row of bobbing dark shapes against the sky. Aunt Liddy followed swiftly, swinging the lighted lantern at her side.

Rainbow was on her way to the landing, too, when she heard Little Willie cry out from his hammock. She hurried to him and picked him up. He clung to her neck and stopped crying at once.

"How sweet you are!" Rainbow told him. "How wonderful it would be if I could take you home with me! You would chase away some of the quiet."

Rainbow held Little Willie close and carried him down to the landing. There was Uncle Whirlwind pulling his loaded canoe on shore. Why, there was Father too! He must have come for her. That moon in the sky was the new moon after all.

Rainbow called to Father, "Glad to see."

At the eating house the men ate hungrily. The

excited cousins lugged bottles of pop and sacks of food from the canoe. But Rainbow sat silently beside Father and snuggled Little Willie to her.

When Uncle Whirlwind asked Father to stay the night, Father answered:

"No, we will leave soon and return home by starlight. Rainbow has been missed. And now we have something to keep her busy."

The grown-ups smiled and looked at Rainbow.

"If only Little Willie could go with me!" Rainbow pleaded. "I know how to take care of him, Aunt Liddy. You have so many children. You won't miss him much. There is no one at our camp for me to play with."

"Some day when he is a little older he will visit you," Aunt Liddy promised.

On the way home Rainbow sat in the middle of the canoe with all the bundles of cloth and the boxes. That biggest box was sure to be her new sewing machine.

"I'll make dolls," Rainbow thought. "I'll make dresses for them on my new machine and sell them for money. But first I'll make a shirt of a thousand pieces for Little Willie. But, oh, how I'll miss him."

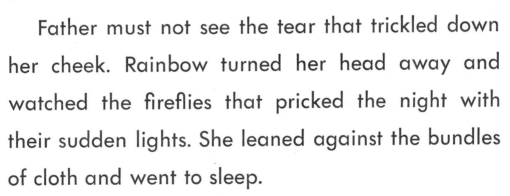

Father must not see the tear that trickled down her cheek. Rainbow turned her head away and watched the fireflies that pricked the night with their sudden lights. She leaned against the bundles of cloth and went to sleep.

Rainbow was wakened by the scraping of the

canoe when Father pulled it on shore at the Jumper camp.

He was grinning. "Get the sleep out of your eyes, little owl," he said. "You are to have a big surprise."

He took that large box from the canoe and started off toward their family *chickee*. Rainbow ran along beside him.

The first morning light was just moving across the sky, drowning out the stars. It was early for the Jumper camp to be awake. Yet the Grandmothers were both with Mother in her *chickee*. They all stood laughing and talking together.

They were so interested in something that they never heard Rainbow and Father until he set the box down with a plop on the *chickee* platform.

"Glad to see." They laughed and crowded around the big package. Father broke loose the string that tied it.

Rainbow stood on tiptoe to see. "Will it be a full sized sewing machine like Mother's?" she wondered. "Oh! Maybe it will be a special small size for me."

Father opened the flaps of the box and lifted out— a little red wagon.

What a strange ending to the mystery! How could a red wagon keep her hands busy? Rainbow didn't have to pretend she was surprised. She was.

Big Grandmother pushed the wagon back and forth on the floor. "Time will race by," she said. "He will soon be big enough to play with it."

"It isn't for me?" asked Rainbow.

Father lifted her high in the air and stood her on the platform.

Mother put her arm around Rainbow and said, "No, little one, the wagon is not for you. But we have something else that will fill your heart with gladness."

Big Grandmother moved aside so Rainbow could see something that took the words from her tongue and the breath from her body. There in a hammock lay a tiny baby with eyes tight shut.

"Is he ours?" Rainbow whispered.

"Your brother, Little Buffalo," said Mother.

Little Buffalo's arms and legs began to beat the air. His mouth opened wide and out came a loud wail, "A-WAH! A-WAH! A-WAH!" He filled the camp with his noise.

Mother picked him up and put him in Rainbow's

arms. He stopped crying and opened eyes as black as watermelon seeds.

"I never guessed you were the mystery," Rainbow told him. "You are the one who will keep my hands busy. You are new—oh, how I'll treasure you, Little Buffalo. You can make so much more noise than a sewing machine."

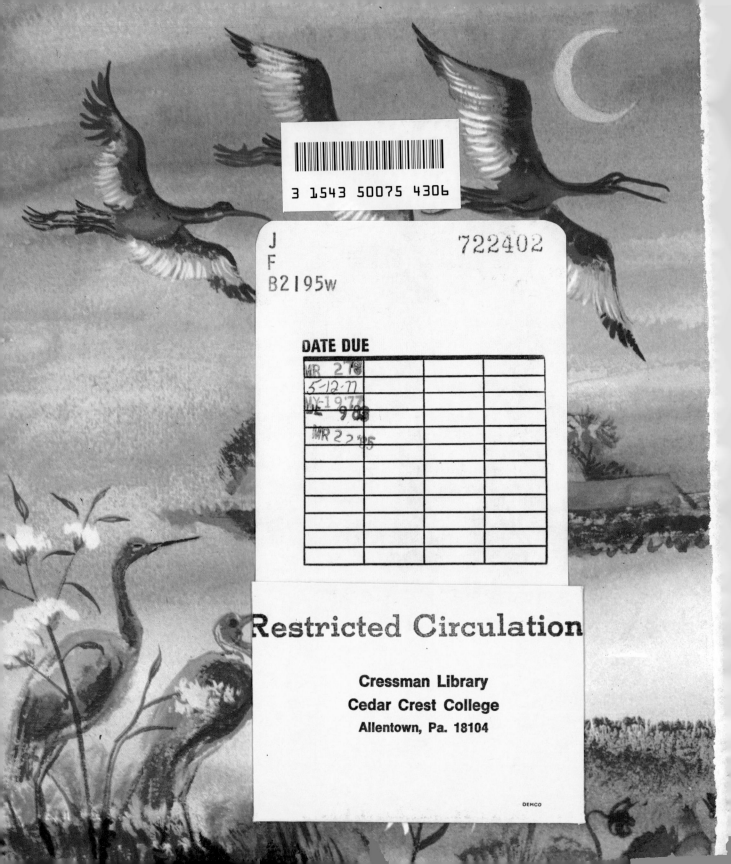